The Boxcar Child

THE CAMP-OUT MYSTERY

created by
GERTRUDE CHANDLER WARNER

Illustrated by Charles Tang

SCHOLASTIC INC.
New York Toronto London Auckland Sydney

ISBN 0-590-45374-2

24 23   4 5 6 7 8 9/0

Printed in the U.S.A.   40

First Scholastic printing, April 1992

Contents

CHAPTER 1

Going Camping

"Do we have everything?" Grandfather Alden asked.

The four Alden children looked inside the station wagon. They had gotten up before dawn to pack for their camping trip. Five backpacks, one for Grandfather and one for each of the children, lay side by side. Each contained a sleeping bag, extra clothes, and a flashlight. Next to the bags were two folded tents and a cooler.

Their dog, Watch, stood on his hind legs and put his front paws on the tailgate so he could see, too. Everyone laughed.

"Don't worry, Watch," Benny, the youngest Alden, said. "I packed your food dish."

The dog's food and dishes were packed in his own special backpack. Jessie had made it for him out of an old piece of canvas.

Jessie lifted the top of the cooler. An old frying pan, stew pot, tablecloths, and dishes were packed inside.

"Is my cup in there?" Benny asked. It was right on top. No matter where he went, he always took his cracked pink cup. It was special to him. He had found it in the dump back when the children lived in the boxcar.

Violet checked her list. "What about the lantern?" she asked.

"I packed it," fourteen-year-old Henry said. "Extra batteries, too."

"Do we need a camping stove, Grandfather?" Jessie asked.

"No," Grandfather answered. "The camp provides places to make fires for cooking."

"If they didn't, we could build one," Benny said. He was six years old and a good helper.

"I guess that's everything," Violet said.

"Okay, Watch," Jessie directed her dog. "Hop in."

Watch jumped into the wagon, turned around three times, and curled up on top of a tent.

Grandfather closed the station wagon's back door. "Well, then, we're on our way."

Henry and Violet climbed into the backseat. Jessie sat in the front and opened the map. Grandfather had marked the route for her.

Benny hung back. "Wait!" he said. "Where's our lunch?" Food was Benny's favorite thing.

Jessie glanced behind her. The picnic basket was not there. "And the trail mix," she said. "We forgot the trail mix." Benny and Violet had made the blend of nuts and dried fruit the day before.

Benny started running toward the house "I'll get it," he said.

Just then, Mrs. McGregor came toward them. She carried the basket and two paper bags.

"We almost forgot the most important thing," Benny said.

Mrs. McGregor laughed. "I couldn't let you do that." She handed Benny the bags.

"This bag feels warm," Benny said.

"Your favorite cookies — just out of the oven," Mrs. McGregor explained. She handed the picnic basket through the window to Henry.

Benny climbed in beside Violet.

Grandfather started the car. "I don't know what we'd do without you, Mrs. McGregor," he said.

Mrs. McGregor stepped back. "Have a good time," she said and waved.

The children waved to her. "See you next week," they all called.

Outside Silver City, they picked up speed. Watch nudged Benny over a bit and put his nose out the window.

Benny laughed. "Watch wants to see where we're going, too," he said.

"There's another reason a dog hangs its head out a car window," Violet said. She liked animals and was always reading about them. "A dog gets nervous in a moving car. When he's nervous, he sweats. But he doesn't sweat like we do; he salivates."

Benny was just about to ask what *salivate* meant when Violet explained.

"He gets lots of saliva in his mouth and then — "

"He drools," Benny said.

Violet nodded. "But with his head out the window, he gets better air circulation," she said. "He cools off, stops sweating, and feels better."

Benny liked his explanation better. Why wouldn't Watch want to see where he was going? It was fun to see the landscape change. In just a few miles, everything looked different. The houses got further and further apart. Instead of busy towns, small quiet farms dotted the hillsides.

Violet started to hum. Before long, everyone was singing: "*A-camping we will go. A-camping we will go . . .* "

After a while, Benny stopped singing. "I'm hungry," he said. "Can we stop somewhere and have our picnic?"

The others agreed that might be a good idea. They were all getting hungry.

"There used to be a nice roadside picnic area along here somewhere," Mr. Alden said.

Jessie pointed to a sign. It said: *Picnic Area 1/4 Mile*. "Is that the one?" she asked.

"It must be," Mr. Alden said as they approached the small picnic grove. He pulled off the road and parked the car. Everyone piled out. Watch ran around sniffing the ground.

The place was a mess. Empty cans and paper lay all around.

Mr. Alden shook his head. "It doesn't look like the same place," he said. "It was always so clean."

"Let's clean it up," Henry said. He began picking up cans and throwing them into the garbage can. Violet and Mr. Alden helped. Watch thought it was a game. He began bringing cans to them.

Benny found a small branch which he used like a broom to sweep off a picnic table. "That's the best I can do," he said.

"It's clean enough," Jessie said. "We have

a tablecloth." She opened the picnic basket. Inside was the blue cloth Henry had bought when they lived in the boxcar.

Jessie spread the cloth over the table and laid out paper plates and cups. She placed a wrapped sandwich on each plate: peanut butter for Benny and Grandfather Alden; tuna for Henry and Violet; cheese for herself. Violet gave each some potato chips and an apple. Henry poured milk from the thermos into paper cups.

They all sat down on the picnic benches and began eating their lunches.

"I think you'll like the campgrounds," Mr. Alden said. "I certainly enjoyed camping there when I was your age."

"Did you camp there often?" Henry asked.

"Quite often," Grandfather answered. "Camping was my parents' favorite vacation. Of course, very few people camped then. Now, it's a big thing — everyone goes camping."

"Do you suppose it'll be crowded?" Violet asked.

Mr. Alden shrugged. "Might be. This *is* spring vacation."

"Maybe we won't get in," Benny said.

"We'll get in," Mr. Alden assured him. "I made a reservation. In the old days, we didn't have to do that. We'd just pack up and off we'd go."

Back in the car, Jessie studied the map. "I think we turn up ahead," she directed.

"Sure enough," Grandfather said. "There're the old cottonwood trees."

At the corner, four large trees grew side by side. A road sign stood across from them. It read: *County B*. Mr. Alden made a smooth turn onto the unpaved road.

"Hang onto your hats," he said. "This is a bumpy one."

The children bounced as the car hit a hole in the road. They drove along the curving road for several miles. Finally, they saw a big wooden sign.

"*Blue Mound State Park*," Benny read. "We're here!"

Grandfather Alden laughed. "And now, the adventure begins!"

CHAPTER 2

Stocking Up

A grocery store stood near the entrance to the forest preserve.

"There's no store inside the park," Mr. Alden said. "We'll do our shopping here."

His tail wagging, Watch followed them to the door.

"You can't come in," Benny told him.

"Sit," Jessie said.

Watch sat.

Jessie put out her hand. "Stay," she said.

Watch cocked his head. He seemed to be saying, "I'll wait, but I don't like it."

The woman behind the counter greeted them. "Welcome," she said.

"Doris?" Grandfather asked.

The woman looked puzzled. "Yes, I'm Doris, but I don't — "

Mr. Alden put out his hand. "James Henry Alden," he said.

The woman smiled and shook his hand. "James! How nice to see you."

"It's been a long time," he replied.

"Too long," she said.

"These are my grandchildren," he said proudly. "This is Henry James. He's the oldest. He's in charge of food for the trip."

Henry smiled and held up his shopping list. "Grandfather told us we could get everything we needed here."

"Then there's Jessie," Grandfather continued. "She's twelve and in charge of the map for our camping trip."

Jessie said "Hello."

"Violet is our musician," Grandfather said. "She's only ten, but you should hear her play the violin."

Violet smiled shyly.

"It's always good to have a little music in the woods," Doris said.

"And I'm Benny," the littlest Alden said. "I'm six. I help with everything."

"I'm happy to know such good campers," Doris said.

"So, Doris, are the campgrounds crowded?" Mr. Alden asked.

"No. Things have been slow lately," Doris said. "Camping isn't what it used to be."

"How's your sister?" Mr. Alden asked. "Hildy — was that her name?"

"Yes, Hildy," Doris said. She glanced away. "She's — uh — fine."

"I remember the two of you — "

"I'd rather not talk about Hildy," Doris interrupted.

"Oh, I'm sorry," Mr. Alden said. "I hope she isn't ill."

Ignoring that, Doris came around the counter. "Let's see that shopping list," she said to Henry. "You probably want to get a move on."

They piled the groceries on the counter: bread, peanut butter, jam, milk, eggs, pancake mix, syrup, crackers, cheese, hot dogs, cooked chicken, fresh vegetables, and fruit — all the things they would need for a few days in the woods.

"The marshmallows," Benny reminded them.

"And the graham crackers and chocolate bars," Violet added.

"And the ice," Henry said.

"The ice machine is outside," Doris said.

Henry ran to get a bag. He brought it and the cooler back into the store.

They unpacked the cooler and put in the ice and the perishable items. The remaining groceries, along with the dishes and cooking things, went into two boxes.

Doris followed them to the door. "I hope nothing . . . spoils the trip for you," she said.

"I'm sure we'll have a wonderful time," Mr. Alden said as he put the boxes into the wagon.

Driving away, they waved to Doris, who was still standing in the doorway.

"What did she mean she hoped nothing would spoil our trip?" Henry asked.

"And not wanting to talk about her sister — that was strange," Jessie said.

"She was so friendly at first," Violet put in. "And then, suddenly . . ."

Mr. Alden nodded. "She did act strangely. Not at all the way I remember her."

"What was her sister like?" Violet asked.

"Hildy didn't like people very much," Mr. Alden replied. "She liked going off by herself. She lived in a cabin at the edge of the woods. The family owned it. They used it as a vacation hideaway until Hildy grew up. Then, she moved into it full time. Still, Doris and Hildy were always close." He shook his head. "It sure is a mystery," he said.

Benny sighed. "I hope not," he said.

The children laughed. They knew exactly what he meant. They liked mysteries. They were good at solving them. But they were looking forward to a peaceful camping trip with no mystery to think about.

CHAPTER 3

Checking In

Mr. Alden stopped the car just inside the park's entrance. "We have to sign in," he said.

Henry pointed to a big wooden arrow on a post. The word *Campers* was carved into it. "The arrow says campers should go to the right," Henry told him.

"I know," Mr. Alden said, "but I'm sure the ranger's station was to the left last time I was here."

"Maybe they moved it?" Benny asked.

Mr. Alden turned the car to the right. "There's only one way to find out," he said.

They drove along the unpaved road slowly. Half a mile in, the road ended.

"I guess we should have turned left," Benny said.

"Right you are," Mr. Alden agreed. He drove around the circle and headed the car back the way they had come.

When they came to the arrow, Henry said, "Stop the car, Grandfather. I'll turn the sign around."

Mr. Alden slowed to a stop.

Henry got out. He had to stretch to reach the arrow.

"Who do you suppose pointed the sign the wrong way?" Jessie asked when Henry was back in the car.

"The nail that attaches it to the post is loose," Henry said. "Maybe it just slipped around the other way."

"Could it slip that far by itself?" Violet asked.

"Violet's right," Jessie said. "If it slipped, it would point down."

"Or up," Benny put in.

"Maybe a strong wind blew it all the way around," Henry offered.

"It was probably someone playing a joke," Mr. Alden said.

Just ahead, they saw a freshly painted, green guard house. Avoiding a stack of old boards near it, Mr. Alden pulled up to the window.

The man inside the house wore a brown uniform with a state park insignia on the pocket. He smiled broadly. "Welcome to Blue Mound State Park," he said.

"We're the Aldens," Grandfather said. "I called ahead to reserve a campsite."

The man checked their name off his list. Then he handed Mr. Alden a map of the grounds. "You can have your pick of sites," he said.

Mr. Alden gave the map to Jessie. "It's your trip," he said to the children. "You choose the place."

Jessie turned in her seat so that her sister and brothers could see the map. It clearly showed the numbered campsites. Several were clustered in a clearing. Others stood alone in different parts of the woods. They quickly agreed on a location near a stand of pine with a brook running alongside. It reminded them of the place where they had found their boxcar.

Jessie pointed to the spot on the map. "May we camp here?" she asked the ranger.

"It's yours," the man answered.

"We didn't expect a choice," Mr. Alden said to the ranger. "We thought the campgrounds would be crowded. This is usually a busy time, isn't it?"

The ranger's smile faded. He looked toward the woods. "It has been, yes," he said. "In the past."

"Maybe people are getting lost," Benny said. He told the ranger about the sign.

"I'll have to check that out," the man said. He smiled again. "Well, you're all set. I hope you enjoy your stay here."

The Aldens thanked him and drove on to the parking lot beyond the guard house.

"I'm glad we're finally here," Benny said. "I'm hungry."

Jessie laughed. "It'll be a while before we eat," she said.

"Yes," Violet agreed. "We have to take everything to our campsite first."

"And set it up," Henry added.

Benny hopped out of the car. "Well, let's hurry," he said. Mr. Alden opened the back of the station wagon and Watch jumped out. His tail wagged wildly. He was obviously happy to be out of the car.

Each of the Aldens slipped on a backpack.

Jessie knelt beside Watch. She put his pack on his back and wound the straps under and over him. He stood very still. When she had buckled the straps, he turned his head to look at the pack. Then, he glanced up at her.

She laughed. "If you're going to go camping," she told him, "you have to carry your own load."

"There's still a lot to carry," Henry said. "We might have to make two trips."

Mr. Alden studied the map. "It's a long hike to our campsite," he said. "If we have to make two trips, it might be dark before we're settled."

"We'll each carry something," Benny suggested.

"The groceries are heavy," Henry said. "I don't think it'll work."

"Come with me, Henry," Jessie directed. "I have an idea."

The others waited while the two oldest ran back to the ranger's house. Shortly, they returned carrying a board.

"The ranger said we could use this," Jessie said. "It's an old board from one of the park buildings. They've been making repairs."

Henry set a box near each end of the board. The tents and their other things went in between.

"That should work," Jessie said. "The weight is even."

"Who wants to help me carry the board?" Henry asked.

"I will," Mr. Alden said.

"Violet and I will carry the cooler," Jessie suggested.

"What about me?" Benny asked. "I can carry something."

"Would you carry my violin?" Violet asked.

Benny beamed and took the case from her. "I'll be very careful with it," he said.

Violet smiled at him. "I know you will, Benny," she said.

Single file, they started off down the path to their campsite. Watch took the lead. He ran ahead, his nose to the ground. Every so often, he would stop and look back to make sure the others were coming.

The air was clear and cool. High above them, birds sang. They passed through a stand of pine. The pine needles were soft underfoot. They could hear the murmur of rushing water.

"We're nearly there," Henry announced.

And sure enough, on the other side of the pine grove was a small clearing. A perfect setting except for the cans and paper bags and plastic cups and tableware.

"Somebody must have been camping here recently," Jessie said.

"And it looks like they left in a hurry," Benny said.

CHAPTER 4

Making Camp

The Aldens put down their burdens and stared at the mess.

"Why would anyone leave a campsite like this?" Violet asked.

"Thoughtlessness," Mr. Alden answered. "People don't think about the effect they have on the environment."

Henry slid off his backpack and set it on the ground. Then, he leaned over and picked up a soda can. Following his lead, everyone chose a spot to clean up. Before long, the campsite was cleared of debris, and the garbage pail under the maple tree was nearly filled.

"Now, we can make camp," Henry said.

"The first thing to do is decide where the cooking and dining areas will be," Mr. Alden said.

Jessie walked over to a circle of large stones. Charred wood lay inside. Nearby, there was a picnic table. "How's this?" she asked.

"Perfect," Mr. Alden said.

Henry and Benny unrolled a flat piece of canvas to protect their supplies from the weather. While it was spread on the ground, they fastened the six tent poles, four to the ends and two in the middle. Next, Henry found a large stone and pounded six pegs into the ground. Then, he tied a line that extended from the top of each pole to a peg.

"Okay," he said. "Time to put up the tent."

The children raised the first two corner poles.

"Hold them steady," Henry directed as he tightened the lines.

They moved to the opposite corner and did the same. When the middle two poles were standing, the job was finished.

"Good job," Mr. Alden said, "but not quite right."

"What's wrong with it, Grandfather?" Benny asked.

"It's flat," Mr. Alden pointed out. "What will happen if it rains?"

"The water will pool on top," Henry said.

"And probably leak through," Jessie added.

"I know what to do," Henry said. He picked up his pounding rock and began driving a corner peg deeper into the ground. He did the same to three other corner pegs but not to the center two poles. When he had finished, the canvas sloped down from the middle. Now, water would run off of it.

Next, they had to choose a spot for their sleeping tent.

"How about under that tree?" Benny asked. "It'll be nice and shady."

"It would be cool there," Grandfather agreed, "but if it storms — "

"Lightning," Violet said.

"How about right here where I'm standing?" Mr. Alden asked.

The children examined the spot. It was clear — no rocks or roots or poison ivy beds — and it sloped just enough so that rain would run down and not pool.

"It's a good place for our tent," Henry said.

Watch pawed the ground. Benny squatted beside him. He saw a mound of earth with small holes in it.

"The ants thought it was a good place, too," he said. "I don't want to spoil their home."

They decided on another location nearer the brook. While Mr. Alden and the boys pitched the tent, Jessie and Violet began unpacking supplies under the canvas covering the cooking area.

"We can't just put things on the ground," Violet said.

"No," Jessie agreed. "Everything will get damp and ruined."

They gathered big rocks and made two

stacks several feet apart. These they bridged with the old park building board. It was a perfect table for the supply boxes and the first aid kit. The cooler fit underneath with room to open the lid.

The boys had done a good job, too. The sleeping tent was up and the backpacks and sleeping bags were inside.

"Now can we eat?" Benny asked.

"First we have to collect wood for a fire," Henry said.

Benny ran over to the cooking pit. "There's wood here." He pointed to a small woodpile nearby.

"I suppose that's enough for tonight," Henry said. "We'll gather more in the morning."

"You make the fire," Jessie said to Henry and Mr. Alden. "We'll find some long sticks for the hot dogs." She, Benny, and Violet ran off into the woods.

Henry made a wood teepee in the center of the pit and stuffed some newspaper inside. Mr. Alden got the matches from the tin box in the kitchen tent.

By the time the girls and Benny returned, the fire was burning nicely, and Henry had made a salad of lettuce, tomatoes, and shredded cheese, and set the picnic table.

The Aldens roasted their hot dogs.

"I'm going to put my salad on mine," Benny said. He tore some lettuce into small pieces and cut up a tomato slice. He piled them and a spoonful of cheese on his bun.

"That's a good idea," Grandfather said, doing the same.

"Save room for Mrs. McGregor's cookies," Jessie reminded everyone.

"I always have room for those!" Benny assured her.

After supper, everyone cleaned up.

"We can burn the paper plates and napkins in the fire," Henry said.

"And if we put the wet garbage at the outer edge of the fire," Jessie said, "we can burn it when it dries."

Finished with the cleanup, they sat around the fire.

"Let's tell ghost stories," Henry suggested but everyone was too tired to think of one.

Benny felt something whiz past him. He ducked. "What was *that*?" he asked.

"I think it was a bat," Henry said. He pointed upward where small dark shapes swooped.

"They're out catching insects for their supper," Mr. Alden said. "They'll be gone soon."

"It almost hit me!" Benny said.

"Oh, it wouldn't do that," Grandfather assured him. "Bats have a very good sense of direction."

"They have a kind of radar," Violet told him. "They bounce sound off objects to locate them."

"Just so *they* don't bounce off *me*!" Benny said.

They all laughed.

Bright stars filled the sky. Everyone leaned back to admire them.

Using his jacket for a pillow, Benny settled against a tree trunk. "I think I'll stay up all night and look at the stars," he decided. But he had no sooner said that than his eyes closed, and in a minute he was asleep.

CHAPTER 5

Loud Dreams

Violet awoke with a start. She thought she had heard something. She sat up in her sleeping bag. On the other side of the tent, Watch was alert, his ears up, listening. Violet seemed to be the only one of the Aldens in the big tent who was awake. She got up and peeked outside. The woods were wrapped in mist.

Jessie came up behind Violet. "What's the matter?" she asked her sister.

"I thought I heard something," Violet said. She and Jessie started toward the dining tent.

"Music?" Jessie asked.

"Loud music," Violet answered. "Did you hear it, too?"

Jessie nodded. "I thought I was dreaming. Where do you suppose it was coming from?"

Violet shook her head. "I don't know. At first, I thought it was someone's radio — another camper's maybe. But it kept getting louder. It seemed to be coming from just over there." She pointed toward the trees at the edge of their camp.

"And then it faded," Jessie said. "Maybe someone walked past *carrying* a radio."

"I don't think so," Violet said. "It was too dark to be hiking in the woods."

"Whoever it was might know the woods well," Jessie suggested. "And maybe they had a lantern."

"But why would anyone want to play loud music like that in the middle of the night? Especially if they were hiking in the woods?" Violet wondered.

"To scare animals?" Jessie suggested.

"I don't know," Violet said. "It just doesn't make sense. And I heard something else:

someone or something moving around out here. Watch heard it, too."

"Well, it's quiet now," Jessie said.

"And it's getting light," Violet added. "I don't think I can get back to sleep."

"A nice hot shower would feel good," Jessie said.

"Yes," Violet agreed.

While the others slept, Jessie and Violet got out clean clothes and followed the path to the bathhouse. It was a big building divided into two parts: one for men; one for women. Inside each section, a line of sinks faced a line of showers.

When they were dressed in clean jeans and T-shirts, they walked back to camp.

At the site, Henry was up and setting the table. "I used the plastic tablecloth," he said. "I thought we should save the blue one for dinnertime."

Henry put a bowl of fruit on the table next to the lantern. The red apples, yellow bananas, and green grapes made a colorful centerpiece.

Benny brought out the cereal boxes. "I

can't find the honey," he told the others.

"It was in the big box with the cereal and crackers," Jessie said.

Benny shrugged. "I didn't see it there."

Jessie went back to the kitchen tent with him. She glanced into the box, but she didn't see the squeeze bottle of honey either. She lifted everything out and looked inside. "That's strange," she said. "The honey isn't here."

Henry saw something on the ground next to the cooler. He reached down and picked it up. It was the honey.

"How do you suppose it got out of the box?" Jessie wondered aloud.

Benny glanced to either side of him. "Are there bears in these woods?" he asked.

·"It was probably just a raccoon or something," Violet assured him. That would explain the noise she heard.

Mr. Alden emerged from the tent. "Good morning, children," he said. "You're up early."

"Good morning, Grandfather," Jessie and Benny chorused.

"Breakfast is ready," Henry said. "I'm afraid there's no coffee, though. We didn't make a fire to heat the water."

"Orange juice and cereal are just fine," Grandfather said.

They all sat down and poured their favorite cereal into bowls. Benny sliced a banana on top of his cornflakes.

"Did everyone sleep well?" Mr. Alden asked.

"I dreamed I was listening to an orchestra," Henry said. "Suddenly, the music got louder and louder."

Benny looked surprised. "I dreamed about loud music, too," he said.

Violet and Jessie exchanged glances. "That wasn't a dream," Jessie said. "We heard loud music, too!"

"So did I," Mr. Alden put in. "It didn't last long, but it was very disturbing."

"I wonder where it came from," Henry said.

"Some camper with his radio volume turned up," Mr. Alden suggested.

"That's what we thought," Violet said,

"but it got so loud it sounded as though it were near us."

"And then it faded," Jessie added.

"Well, I just hope they don't do that every night," Benny said. "I don't like loud dreams."

Violet and Benny put the napkins and other dry garbage in the center of the fire pit, and put a log on top so it wouldn't blow away. They set the wet garbage at the edge of the pit to dry. They would burn it later.

Jessie and Henry washed off the spoons and knives in the brook.

"We'll heat water later to wash them properly," Jessie said.

"What do you children want to do today?" Mr. Alden asked.

"Go exploring!" they all said at once.

"Run along then," he said.

"Don't you want to come with us, Grandfather?" Violet asked.

Mr. Alden shook his head. "Thank you, no. I think I'd like to stay here and read." He opened a magazine he had brought with him.

"We won't be too long," Jessie said.

"Take all the time you want," Mr. Alden said. "Just don't get lost. The woods can be tricky. They can make a person lose all sense of direction."

Henry held up a silver compass. "We won't get lost with this," he assured their grandfather.

Jessie packed some fruit and trail mix for their trip. Now they were ready to go. Watch followed them to the hiking path.

"You stay here with Grandfather," Jessie told him.

"Take Watch with you," Mr. Alden said. "With him along *and* the compass, I won't worry about you getting lost."

Violet paused to look at the dark buds on the maple tree. She reached up and touched one. It felt like velvet. "These are ready to open," she said. "We've come to the forest at a very good time."

CHAPTER 6

The Missing Lantern

They hiked a long way into the woods. After a while they came to another small clearing. A camp was set up there. A woman, a man, and two small children sat at the picnic table eating breakfast. At one end of the table, a portable radio played softly.

"Maybe they played the loud music," Benny said.

"Let's find out," Henry suggested.

The man saw the Alden children. He snapped off the radio. Then, he waved.

"Hello, there," he said. "Are you camping here, too?"

The Aldens walked closer.

Henry said, "Yes, our camp is over that way." He pointed toward their campsite.

"We're the Changs," the man said. "It's nice to meet you."

Henry introduced himself and his sisters and brother.

"And this is our dog Watch," Benny added.

Watch lifted his paw.

The Chang children giggled.

Mrs. Chang said, "We thought we were the only campers here."

"It seemed a pleasant change," Mr. Chang added. "All the other campgrounds we've tried have been so crowded."

"We thought we were the only ones, too," Benny piped up, "until we heard loud music last night."

The man and woman looked at each other. "Loud music?" they both said.

"You didn't hear it?" Jessie said.

"We were awfully tired last night," Mr.

Chang said. "We slept pretty soundly. But — "

One of the children said, "More milk, Daddy," and reached for the pitcher. It tipped. Mr. Chang caught it just as it was about to fall over.

Just then, the other child slipped off the picnic bench and started to cry. Mrs. Chang rushed to pick her up.

Henry edged toward the path. "We'll see you again," he said.

The Aldens hiked along silently. They listened to the birds singing overhead. They saw chipmunks and squirrels and rabbits.

Finally Jessie said, "It sure is strange that the Changs didn't hear that music last night. Their campsite isn't *that* far from ours."

"Do you think the Changs are the ones who played it?" Violet asked.

"They have a radio," Jessie said. "They could be the ones."

"But why would they do it?" Henry asked.

"I don't know," Jessie answered.

They fell silent again, thinking.

After a while, Benny said, "I'm hungry."

"Again!" Violet said.

"You're *always* hungry," Henry joked.

"I know," Benny agreed.

Jessie pointed to a large flat rock. "Let's sit there," she said, "and eat some fruit."

"We can leave the seeds and peels here," Violet said when they had finished their snack. "The birds and small animals will eat them."

They continued on. Every so often, they found an empty soda can or some other waste. They picked it up and dumped it into their empty lunch sack.

When it was full, Henry said, "Too bad there aren't more garbage cans along the way. We'll have to carry this with us until we find one."

Before long, they came to a wide stream. Watch wagged his tail and lapped up a drink of water.

"This must be the same brook that runs along our campsite," Henry said. He took out the campgrounds map and studied it. "We're nearly out of the park," he told the others. "We'd better turn back."

They followed the stream back toward camp.

"We have to stop for wood," Henry reminded them.

There were special areas marked on the map where campers could get wood. The children stopped at one. They dropped the debris they had collected into a garbage can. Then they went to the large, tarpaulin-covered woodpile.

"How will we carry the wood back to camp?" Violet wondered.

"I have an idea," Henry said. He took off his belt. He wrapped it around several pieces of wood and buckled it. "We can carry it this way."

When the children got back to camp, Grandfather was napping against the maple tree, his magazine open beside him.

The children didn't wake him. Instead, they took off their shoes and socks and went wading in the stream. The cold clear water soothed their tired feet. They splashed it on their wrists and faces. It was refreshing.

* * *

In the late afternoon, Henry and Benny laid the fire. Then they went into the kitchen tent to prepare supper.

"Benny, you can peel and slice the carrots," Henry directed. "Jessie, you do the potatoes." He began slicing a large onion.

Grandfather came in. "What can I do?" he asked.

"You can tear up the lettuce for the salad," Violet said. "I'll set the table."

When they all had finished, Violet made hamburger patties and Henry put each one into a foil packet with some of the vegetables. Jessie lit the fire. "We don't want a big flame for this meal," Henry said. "We'll have to let it burn down a while."

While they waited for the fire to be just right, they sat at the table and had cranberry juice and crackers.

"How was your hike?" Mr. Alden asked.

"We met some other campers," Henry said.

"They didn't hear the loud music," Violet told him.

"That's strange," Mr. Alden said. "It was

loud enough to be heard all over the park."

"That's what we thought," Jessie said.

"They must be very sound sleepers," Mr. Alden said.

When most of the logs had turned to ash, Henry brought out the foil packages and Jessie set them on top of the coals. Twenty minutes after that, everyone sat down to enjoy their meal.

"This is delicious," Jessie said.

Everyone agreed.

"It's called hobo stew," Henry said.

"What are we having for dessert?" Benny asked.

"Who needs dessert after that big meal?" Grandfather teased.

"I do," Benny said.

Jessie brought out the marshmallows, graham crackers, and chocolate bars. Violet got the long, pointed sticks. Henry added wood to the fire. Benny danced around it excitedly.

"S'mores!" he exclaimed. "My favorite."

They sat around the campfire until it had burned itself out. Even then, they hated to go to bed.

"It's so quiet here," Violet said.

"And so dark," Benny added.

"I'll get the lantern," Henry said. He walked to the table. Then he called, "Where *is* the lantern?"

"The last time I saw it, it was on the table," Jessie said. It was there when Violet and I came back from our showers."

"It was there after breakfast," Violet said. "I had to move it when I took off the tablecloth."

"Then it must have been there when we left for our hike," Henry said. He made his way to the tent where he got a flashlight from his backpack. He shone it this way and that, but he couldn't find the lantern anywhere. "Someone must have taken it," he concluded.

"Why would anyone want our lantern?" Benny asked.

"How could anyone have taken it?" Mr. Alden wondered. "I was here the whole time you were gone. Do you think someone took it while I dozed?"

"Maybe," Jessie said.

"Wherever it is, we won't find it tonight," Mr. Alden said. "It's time to turn in. We'll look for it in the morning."

Suddenly Watch, who had been curled up at Jessie's feet, sat up. He growled softly.

"What is it, Watch?" Jessie asked.

"Look over there!" Benny said. "Lights!"

They all looked toward the woods. Two beams of light moved away from them. They seemed to dance through the trees. Then, just as suddenly as they had appeared, they were gone.

"What was *that*?" Benny asked.

"Maybe it's someone with our lantern," Violet answered.

"There were *two* light beams," Henry said.

"It could be people with flashlights," Jessie said. "The Changs maybe."

"What would they be doing in the woods at this time of night?' Violet asked.

Jessie couldn't think of a single reason.

Mr. Alden got to his feet. "Let's sleep on it," he said. "In daylight, things look less mysterious."

CHAPTER 7

No Pancakes for Breakfast

Next morning, Henry had the fire going by the time the others woke up. They were all surprised.

"If we had something to put the frying pan on, we could have pancakes for breakfast," Jessie said.

"We do have something," Henry told her.

Resting on two stacks of stones, a metal grill spanned the fire.

"Watch and I went looking for our lantern this morning," Henry explained. "I thought some animal might have carried it off and dropped it somewhere. Instead, we found the grill at an empty campsite."

Violet said, "Now you can have your coffee, Grandfather." Then she and Benny skipped off to fill the coffee pot with water from the pump.

Jessie went to make the pancake batter. The mix wasn't in the box. She looked all over for it. Finally, she returned to the others. "I can't find the pancake mix," she told them.

"Are you sure we bought some?" Henry asked her.

"Yes," Jessie answered. "It was in the box with the cereal."

"Maybe Benny moved it when he was looking for the honey," Mr. Alden suggested.

"I looked in both boxes. I even looked in the cooler," Jessie said. "It's not anywhere."

Returning with the coffee pot, Violet asked, "What's missing now?"

"The pancake mix," Jessie told her.

"Oh, no," Benny said. "Not the pancake mix!"

"Something strange is going on," Mr. Alden said thoughtfully.

"There's probably a simple explanation for everything that's happened," Henry said.

"A raccoon could have taken the pancake mix," Jessie said, "and knocked the honey out of the box."

"He might even have carried the lantern off somewhere," Violet added.

"That could explain the light," Benny put in. "Maybe he was running with the lantern and the light was bouncing all over the place."

"That *could* make it look like two lights when it was only one," Henry said.

"And who turned the lantern on?" Grandfather asked.

"Raccoons are very smart," Benny answered.

"Smart enough to play music?" Mr. Alden asked.

"There wasn't any music last night," Violet said.

"No," Mr. Alden said, "but I don't think we've heard the last of it."

Everyone was silent thinking about that.

Finally, Henry said, "I don't think we're in any danger."

"No, I don't think we are," Grandfather agreed, "but I'm not sure we should stay."

"Oh, please, let's not go home yet, Grandfather," Benny pleaded.

Mr. Alden looked from one to the other. "Do you all want to stay?"

"Oh, yes!" the children all said at once.

"All right," Mr. Alden said at last. "But I'm going to hike back to the store for another lantern."

"We could do that," Henry offered.

"Thank you, Henry," Mr. Alden said, "but the walk would do me good, and I'd like to talk to Doris. You stay here and enjoy the woods."

After a breakfast of scrambled eggs, Henry packed some trail mix and fruit and a thermos of coffee for Mr. Alden.

"How nice of you to pack me a lunch," Grandfather told him, "but I'll only be gone a little while."

"You'd better take it, Grandfather," Benny said. "Hiking makes a person very hungry."

Mr. Alden started toward the trail. Watch looked confused. He didn't seem to know whether to go with him or to stay with the children.

Mr. Alden laughed. "You stay here, Watch. I'll be back soon."

Watch wagged his tail. He seemed to understand.

The children decided to play hide and seek in the pine grove. Henry covered his eyes and began to count. Everyone else ran to hide. Watch followed Jessie. She found the perfect hiding place under an outcrop of sandstone.

"Shhh," she warned Watch.

The dog sat quietly beside her.

Still, Henry found them. He found Benny and Violet, too.

"So who wants to be It now?" Henry asked.

"It's too hot to play," Benny said. "Let's go wading instead."

They took off their shoes and socks and rolled up their jeans. The children laughed and splashed in the cool stream for a long time. Then they dried off in the sun.

"Let's make stew for supper," Jessie suggested. "Grandfather will be hungry after his long hike."

Jessie got the fire going.

Benny took the stew pot to the pump to fill it with water.

Henry and Violet cut up the vegetables and chunks of beef.

By the time the stew was simmering, the sky was dark with clouds.

"It looks like we're in for a storm," Henry observed.

"I hope Grandfather gets back soon," Jessie said.

Lightning flashed in the distance. After several seconds, a low rumble sounded. An hour later, the first big drops of rain fell on their camp.

But Grandfather Alden had not returned.

CHAPTER 8

The Storm

"What do you suppose happened to Grandfather?" Benny asked.

They had pulled the picnic table under the kitchen tent and were sitting at it. Rain fell all around them. In the distance, thunder rumbled. Plates of stew sat before them. No one was very hungry.

"I'm sure he's all right," Jessie said. She didn't want the others to know how worried she was.

"It's not safe to be walking in the woods during a storm," Henry reminded them.

"Grandfather probably decided to stay with Doris and her family."

"Yes," Jessie said. "That's what he did. He stayed with Doris."

"He'll be here by the time we get up in the morning," Violet added. But she was as worried as Jessie.

"Then let's go to bed now," Benny suggested, "so morning will come quicker. I don't like being here without Grandfather."

They put the leftover stew in a container in the cooler and cleared off the table.

Henry aimed his flashlight at the big tent. The others made a dash for it. When they were safely inside, he ran to join them.

Their sleeping bags felt warm and cozy, but they couldn't sleep. They lay listening to the rain drumming on the tent, each of them thinking about Grandfather. His empty sleeping bag made them feel even sadder.

After a long silence, Henry said, "Remember when we didn't want to live with Grandfather?"

"Yes, we thought he was mean," Violet said.

"And we didn't even know him!" Jessie put in.

"That wasn't very smart," Benny summed up. "He's the best grandfather in the whole world."

Suddenly, everything was light and sound. Lightning flashed. Thunder crashed. The ground shook. The children moved closer together. Benny pulled his sleeping bag up over his head.

The storm pounded around them for most of the night. When it finally moved on, Benny sighed. "I'm glad it's over," he said. He rolled over and went to sleep.

The others were just drifting off when — suddenly — music ripped through the night air.

Watch pricked up his ears. He stood up, listening. Then he moved to the tent flap and poked his nose outside.

"What is it, boy?" Henry whispered. "Who's out there?"

Watch looked at Henry over his shoulder. He yawned, turned around three times, and curled up by the door of the tent.

"The music sounds close," Jessie whispered.

"It's even louder than last time," Violet added.

Then, just as suddenly as it had started, the music stopped. The rain had stopped, too. Except for the steady *drip drip* from the trees, everything was quiet.

"Whoever's playing it doesn't want us here," Henry said.

"What makes you think that?" Jessie asked.

"Why else would they keep playing it at night like they do? And so near?" Henry said. "They're trying to spoil things for us."

" 'I hope nothing spoils the trip for you,' " Violet quoted. "Isn't that what Doris said?"

"Do you suppose she's the one who's trying to scare us off?" Jessie wondered.

"She can't be," Henry said. "She's probably with Grandfather right now."

"I hope so," Jessie said. "I hope he's warm and safe just like we are."

CHAPTER 9

Grandfather Is Missing

Jessie felt something on her arm. Half asleep, she brushed it away. She felt it again. She opened her eyes. Watch sat beside her, pawing her gently.

She sat up. "What is it, Watch? What's the matter?" she whispered.

The dog crept to the tent door where he stood with his head cocked, listening.

Jessie crawled out of her sleeping bag and tiptoed over to him. She lifted the tent flap and went outside, Watch at her side.

Henry came outside. "What's the matter?"

"Watch woke me up," Jessie answered. "I thought someone might be out here. I was hoping it was Grandfather."

"Grandfather would wait until daylight to come back," Henry said. "Watch probably heard the water dripping from the trees."

"Probably," Jessie agreed. Just as she turned to go back inside, she saw something move. "Did you see that?" she whispered.

"What?" Henry said.

She pointed to the edge of their camp. "Something moved over there in the trees."

Henry held up his flashlight. "I don't see anything," he said.

Benny came to the door of the tent rubbing his eyes. "What's going on?" he asked.

"Jessie thought she saw something," Henry told him.

Benny yawned. "It's too dark to see anything," he said and went back inside.

"He's right," Jessie said. "It was probably my imagination."

Henry and Jessie had no sooner gone back to sleep than Benny woke them. "I think we should go find Grandfather," he said.

"Let's have breakfast first," Jessie suggested. "Maybe he'll be here by the time we've finished."

They ate fruit and bread and jelly. They used paper napkins as plates so they wouldn't have to spend time washing dishes.

Afterwards, Henry looked at the map. "The path along the stream is a short cut," he said.

"If we go that way, we might miss Grandfather," Violet objected.

"But Grandfather might still be at Doris's," Jessie said. "It's early. If we take the short cut, we'll be there sooner."

Henry spread out the map. "The shortcut meets the main trail here," he said. "Even if Grandfather starts back, chances are we'll meet up with him."

"What if he comes back and we're not here?" Benny asked. "He'll look for us. We could keep missing one another all day."

"Let's leave a note," Violet suggested. She took a piece of paper and a pencil from their supplies, and wrote: *Went hiking. Back soon.* "How's that?" she asked.

Everyone agreed that was fine. They left the note in the middle of the table. Henry put a rock on it so it wouldn't blow away. Then they all started out of camp.

Benny and Watch ran on ahead. Suddenly, they stopped. The others caught up to them.

"What's the matter?" Henry asked.

Benny put a finger to his lips. He pointed across the stream. There, in the woods, something small and white flicked back and forth through the trees.

"It's a deer!" Violet whispered.

The animal bolted out of sight.

Hoping to see more deer, they kept an eye on the woods as they moved along the trail. Where the stream trail and the main trail met, they saw something else: a cabin.

"I didn't notice that cabin when we hiked to our campsite," Henry said.

Set far back in the thick clump of trees, the log house was easy to miss.

"It's hard to see," Violet said. "It blends into the woods so well."

"It needs a white tail," Benny joked.

Henry started toward it. "Maybe whoever lives there saw Grandfather. Let's ask."

Jessie hesitated. "That says '*No Trespassing.*'" She pointed to an old wooden sign.

Just then a woman came out of the cabin door. She was tall and thin and she was frowning.

"She doesn't look very friendly," Benny whispered.

Moving still closer, Henry called out, "Hello!"

The woman put her hands on her hips and glowered at the children.

"We're looking for our grandfather," Henry told her. "We thought you might have seen him pass by."

"Can you read?" the woman asked.

"Why — uh — yes," Henry said.

"Then why don't you?" she snapped. "'No trespassing' means *no trespassing*."

"Oh, we didn't mean to break any rules," Jessie explained. "We just thought — "

The woman turned on her heel and went back inside the cabin.

"She certainly *is* unfriendly," Henry said.

"You were right about that, Benny."

"Could that be Doris's sister?" Violet wondered aloud.

The others thought about that possibility.

"Grandfather did say she lived in a cabin," Violet reminded them. "And she liked going off by herself."

The main path was full of puddles from the night's rain. Along the sides, earth had been washed down into the gullies. The children picked their way along trying to avoid the mud and deep holes.

The trail headed up the hill. Near the top, Watch pricked up his ears. He sniffed the air. For several seconds, he stood stone still. Suddenly, he broke into a run and disappeared over the crest of the hill.

"What do you suppose he heard?" Violet wondered.

"Whatever it is, he's sure excited about it," Henry said.

"He's probably chasing an animal," Benny offered.

That worried Jessie. Watch was a brave dog, but he was no match for a cornered raccoon or some other wild animal. "Watch!" she called. "Come back!"

Watch came running toward the children. He circled them, yapping excitedly. He took off again. Then he came galloping back to be sure they were following him.

In the lead, Henry picked up his pace. "Come on," he said. "Watch is trying to tell us something."

Forgetting the puddles and the mud, they all raced along the path. At the top of the hill, they looked for Watch. He seemed to have disappeared. But they could hear him barking.

"Watch! Where are you?" Jessie called.

Benny saw something move in the ravine below. He stepped to the edge of the path and looked down. "There he is!" he shouted. "And *Grandfather* is with him!"

CHAPTER 10

Rescuing Grandfather

"Grandfather!" they all said at once.

Mr. Alden was half sitting, half lying under a stone ledge at the bottom of the ravine. Watch stood beside him like a bank guard.

"Are you all right?" Violet called.

"I'm fine," Mr. Alden assured them. "Except for my ankle. I twisted it when I fell."

Henry climbed down the steep slope. The other children followed.

"Be careful," Grandfather warned them. "It's slippery."

"How long have you been here, Grandfather?" Jessie asked.

"All night," Mr. Alden replied.

"Weren't you scared?" Benny asked.

"Well, Benny, I was a little nervous." Then he said, "I don't think I can put any weight on my ankle."

"You can lean on us," Violet said.

Henry slipped Mr. Alden's arm around his neck. "That's right, Grandfather, lean on us."

Jessie and Violet took the other arm.

Mr. Alden shook his head. "Even with your help, I'd never get back up to the path."

Henry looked up toward the trail. It was a hard climb. Grandfather was right, they'd never make it. "We need help," he said.

Benny started up the slope. "Let's hurry!"

"I'll stay with Grandfather," Violet said.

"Watch, you stay, too," Jessie told the dog.

Violet took off her jacket and folded it. "Here, Grandfather, let's put this behind your head."

"You're sure you'll be all right?" Henry asked.

Grandfather nodded. "I'll be fine with Violet and Watch to take care of me."

Back on the trail, Benny said, "Let's get the ranger."

"The cabin is closer," Henry told him.

"But that woman is an old crab," Benny argued. "She won't help us."

"Henry's right, Benny," Jessie said. "Even if the woman won't help us, she might have a telephone. We can call the ranger from there."

They trekked back to the cabin and knocked on the door.

No one answered.

"Please help us," Jessie called. "Our grandfather is hurt!"

. They knocked again. Just as they were about to give up, the cabin door flew open.

"What do you want?!" the woman snapped. "Didn't I tell you to stay away from here?"

"Please let us use your phone," Henry said.

"Telephone!" the woman repeated. "You think I'd have a telephone? What would I want with a telephone?"

"Our grandfather fell down a ravine," Henry said. "We need help to get him out. Could we look around? Maybe you have something we could use to make a stretcher."

"People who can't take care of themselves should stay in the city where they belong!" she shouted. "You need help — go get Andy Watts to help you!" She waved toward the hill behind the cabin and slammed her door.

"Who's Andy Watts?" Benny wondered aloud.

Already running toward the hill, Henry said, "Let's find out."

Beyond the hill, another cabin squatted among the trees.

Henry reached it first. He knocked and called, but no one answered.

"We're wasting time," Jessie said. "Let's head back to the ranger's station."

They were just about to leave when a man carrying a long walking stick came toward them.

He smiled, "Hello, children," he said. "I'm Andy Watts. That's my cabin. What can I do for you?"

"Oh, Mr. Watts, we were looking for you," Henry said. "Our grandfather fell down a ravine and hurt his ankle. We can't get him out. Will you please help us?"

"Of course I'll help you," Mr. Watts said. He hurried into the cabin, saying, "I'll be right back." He came out with a rolled elastic bandage, which he put in his pocket. "Now, show me the way," he said.

The four of them hurried back along the trail.

"How did you know about me?" Mr. Watts asked.

"We went to the other cabin," Jessie told him. "The woman there said a man named Andy Watts would help us."

Mr. Watts nodded. "That's Hildy," he said. "She's something, isn't she?"

"Unfriendly is what she is," Benny said.

Mr. Watts laughed. "Her bark is worse than her bite," he said.

They reached Mr. Alden and Violet and climbed down beside them. Watch got between Mr. Watts and Grandfather. He growled softly.

"That's strange," Jessie observed. "He's usually friendly."

Mr. Watts said, "He's just doing his job — guarding your grandfather." Then he put his hand out toward Watch. The dog sniffed it and wagged his tail. Mr. Watts patted his head. "I like animals," he said, "so they usually like me."

Henry made the introductions, and then Mr. Watts said, "Let me see that ankle." He carefully pulled Mr. Alden's sock down. "It's swollen all right," he said. "Can you move it?"

Grandfather made a slow circle with his foot. "Yes," he said, "but it hurts."

"I don't wonder," Mr. Watts said. "It's a bad sprain. Lucky you didn't break it."

"I thought I did," Mr. Alden told him. "It got twisted under me when I fell."

"How did you fall, Grandfather?" Jessie asked.

"I waited at the store hoping the rain would stop," he said. "When it didn't, I decided to hike back anyway. I was walking along, when suddenly there was a blast of music. It startled me and I slipped. The next thing I knew, I was down here."

"The soil washes away in a heavy rain," Mr. Watts said. "They need to plant more trees along the trail."

"Why don't they do that?" Benny asked. "Then it wouldn't be so dangerous."

"Planting trees costs money," Mr. Watts answered. "People sometimes object to spending their tax money that way."

"They wouldn't if they fell down like Grandfather," Benny said.

Mr. Watts took out the elastic bandage.

"Should I take off Grandfather's shoe?" Violet asked.

"Not until we get him back to camp," the man answered. "His shoe will give him some support." He wrapped the bandage under and over Mr. Alden's shoe and up around his ankle. When he'd tied it securely, he said, "Now, let's get you out of here."

"How will we get Grandfather up the slope?" Henry asked.

"We won't," Mr. Watts answered. "There's a narrow deer path behind this stone outcrop. We'll follow that until the terrain is more even."

Henry and Mr. Watts helped Grandfather up.

"Put this arm around my shoulders," Mr. Watts directed.

"I'll take his other arm," Henry volunteered.

"The path is too narrow for three of us, Mr. Watts said. He gave Mr. Alden his walking stick. "Use this. It'll help."

"I'll carry these," Benny said as he picked up the thermos, and the lantern Grandfather had bought.

"Henry and Violet and I will go on ahead to clear the way," Jessie said.

Mr. Alden and Mr. Watts hobbled along behind them. Before too long, the trail and ravine were just about even.

"We'll go up here," Mr. Watts said.

They started up the slope, but Mr. Alden lost his balance and nearly fell.

"Henry, you and Benny go ahead of Grandfather," Jessie said. "Violet and I will be behind him."

"Good thinking," Mr. Watts said. "Henry and Benny, you take hold of the walking stick. That way you can pull us up."

"And we'll push," Violet said.

With everyone working together, they got Grandfather up the slope to the trail. But it was still a long way back to camp.

"I need to rest," Grandfather said.

"Me, too," Benny piped up.

Mr. Watts helped Mr. Alden to a tree stump. "Stay here and rest," he said. "I'll be back shortly."

When he was gone, Violet said, "Being out in the rain all night must have been awful for you, Grandfather."

"I was able to pull myself under the ledge," Mr. Alden said. "It kept me fairly dry. And I had the new lantern."

"I'll bet you got hungry," Benny put in.

"I had the lunch Jessie made for me," Grandfather reminded him. "I ate every bit of it. And the coffee kept me warm."

Watch barked. Something was moving along the trail toward them. It was Andy Watts, pushing a wheelbarrow. They were surprised to see him back so soon.

"We'll push you back to camp, Mr. Alden," Andy said. "That will make the trip easier for you." He helped Mr. Alden into the barrow.

Grandfather's legs stuck out in a funny way. The children laughed. The men laughed, too.

Henry and Mr. Watts pushed the wheelbarrow along the trail.

"Watch out for bumps!" Grandfather said.

At camp, Benny brought Grandfather's sleeping bag out into the sun. Mr. Watts eased the man onto it. Then he carefully removed his shoe and sock.

"Shall I get an ice pack?" Violet asked.

"That's a good idea," Mr. Watts said.

Violet dashed off to the kitchen tent. There she took ice from the cooler and wrapped it in a plastic bag.

Mr. Watts wrapped the ankle with the elastic bandage. "Keep it elevated," he said. "And stay off of it. It'll probably be fine in a few days."

Violet propped up Grandfather's ankle

with folded clothes and placed the ice pack on it.

"The ice feels good," Mr. Alden said. "Thank you, Violet." He looked around at the others. "Thank you, all!"

Mr. Watts said, "If you need help packing up to leave, just let me know."

"Oh, my ankle will be fine by the time we break camp," Grandfather assured him.

Andy Watts looked surprised. "You mean you aren't going home now?" he asked.

The children looked at Grandfather. They, too, thought he would want to leave. As much as they wanted to stay, they would gladly cut their trip short if Grandfather would be more comfortable at home.

"Oh, no," Mr. Alden said. "My grandchildren are having too good a time. They'll take good care of me, and I can stay off my ankle here as well as at home."

Andy looked doubtful. "Well, I have a feeling you might change you mind," he said. "If you do, you know where to find me." He walked off, pushing the wheelbarrow.

CHAPTER 11

The Note on the Tree

"There goes a good-hearted man," Grandfather said as Andy Watts disappeared into the trees.

"We were lucky to find him," Henry said.

"If it weren't for Doris's sister, we wouldn't have," Jessie said.

Grandfather chuckled. "So you met Hildy."

Benny made a face. "She's so crabby!" he said. "If I were Mr. Watts, I wouldn't live so close to her."

"Andy loves this forest," Grandfather told

them. "There aren't many private cabins in it."

"How do you know so much about him, Grandfather?" Violet asked.

"Doris told me," Mr. Alden explained. "Andy works at the sporting goods store in town. It's a long way, but he likes living close to nature."

"Did Doris tell you anything more about Hildy?" Henry asked.

Grandfather shook his head. "No, not a thing." His eyes closed.

"Grandfather?" Violet said. "Are you all right?"

"Just a little tired."

"I'll bet you're hungry, too," Benny said. "I sure am."

Mr. Alden smiled. "Why don't you children run along and make lunch?" He yawned. "I'll just rest my eyes a bit."

The children ran off to the kitchen tent.

"Mr. Watts said we might change our minds about leaving," Henry commented. "I wonder what he meant."

"Maybe he thinks Grandfather won't be

comfortable here," Violet offered. "His ankle *is* painful."

"But Grandfather wants to stay," Benny put in. "He said so."

"Mr. Watts doesn't know Grandfather," Jessie said.

"That's for sure," Henry added. "He doesn't know that once Grandfather makes up his mind, he doesn't change it easily."

"Henry, you light the fire," Jessie said. "We'll warm up the stew."

Jessie looked into the cooler. She didn't see the container with the stew. "Did you take out the stew when you got the ice?" she asked Violet.

Violet shook her head. "No," she said. "I didn't take out anything but ice."

"Where could it be?" Jessie asked.

The two girls looked all around.

At the table, Violet said. "That's funny. The note we left for Grandfather is gone."

"But you put a stone on it to keep it in place," Jessie said.

"Yes," Violet answered. "Here's the stone, but the note is gone."

Just then, Benny came running up to them. "Come quick," he said.

The girls followed him to the maple tree. Henry stood under it. He pointed. Midway up the trunk was Violet's note.

"The *hiking* and *soon* are scratched out," Jessie observed. "Now it reads: *Went home. Back never.*"

"And look what's holding the note against the tree!" Benny exclaimed.

It was a long, sharp arrow!

Henry reached up and pulled it out of the tree. "Someone is *really* anxious for us to leave," he said.

"But these are campgrounds," Jessie said. "Why would anyone want to keep campers away?"

"We aren't bothering anyone," Violet said.

"Except that nasty Hildy," Benny put in. "Everybody bothers her."

"It doesn't make sense," Jessie said. "Why would Hildy — or anyone — want us to leave?"

"That's what we have to find out," Henry said.

CHAPTER 12

Looking for Clues

They decided not to tell Grandfather about the missing stew and the arrow in the tree.

"It'll only worry him," they all agreed.

Jessie and Benny made sandwiches instead of stew.

After lunch, Grandfather said, "Why don't you children run along. I'm sure you have some more exploring to do."

They wanted to go, but they didn't like the idea of leaving Grandfather alone.

"I'll be fine," he assured them.

Since their return to camp, Watch had stayed by Mr. Alden's side. That gave Jessie an idea. "Watch can stay with you, Grandfather," she suggested.

"There's no need for that," Mr. Alden said. "I'm sure he'd like to be with you children."

Watch pricked up his ears and cocked his head. He looked at the children and then at Mr. Alden. He seemed to be deciding what to do. Finally, he yawned and put his head back on Grandfather's chest.

Everyone laughed.

"I guess that settles that," Grandfather said.

Waving to Grandfather and Watch, the children started off.

Not far from camp, Henry said, "Let's stop here."

"Why?" Benny asked.

"We should talk about what's been happening," Henry explained. "Maybe we can figure out who's responsible."

They made themselves comfortable on a broad stone ledge.

"First we should go back over what's happened," Jessie suggested.

"We've heard music and seen strange lights," Benny piped up.

"The honey wasn't in the box where I'd put it," Jessie said.

"Food's been missing," Henry added. "And our lantern, too."

"Now, my note's been changed and pinned to the tree with an arrow," Violet concluded.

"That about sums it up," Henry said.

"Except for the loud music that startled Grandfather and caused him to fall," Violet said.

"We have to figure out who's doing these things," Jessie said.

"I think it's Hildy," Benny said.

"She *could* be the one," Henry agreed. "She doesn't like people so she might be trying to scare everyone away."

"But there are other people who could be doing it," Jessie said. "The Changs maybe."

"They do have a radio," Henry said.

"And they said they liked this campground

because it wasn't crowded," Violet reminded them. "Maybe they wanted it empty."

"But they have the children," Jessie said. "They wouldn't leave them alone to sneak around stealing food."

"How about Andy Watts?" Henry suggested.

"Not Mr. Watts!" Benny objected. "He's too kind."

"Well, you never know," Jessie argued forcefully.

"He seemed anxious for us to leave," Violet said.

"Only because of Grandfather," Henry said.

"Well, how about the ranger?" Violet suggested. "He probably knows the forest better than anyone. He could get around without being detected."

Henry shook his head. "I don't think he could be the one. If there were no campers, he might lose his job."

Jessie sighed. "It could be someone we don't even know."

"That's right," Henry said. "Maybe there

are campers we don't know about." He got to his feet. "Let's find out."

They followed the map to all the camp-sites. No one was at any of them. Finally, they came to the Changs' spot. Their equipment was there, but the family was not.

"They're probably out hiking," Henry said. "Let's head over toward Hildy's and Andy's. Maybe we'll find some clues."

They doubled back, stopping to check on Grandfather. He was asleep, Watch at his side.

A short distance down the stream trail, Benny saw something. He ran ahead to see what it was. Partially hidden in a clump of bushes was the wheelbarrow.

"Why would Mr. Watts leave that here?" Violet wondered aloud.

"Maybe it's not his," Henry said. "It could belong to the park staff."

"Or maybe he was too tired after helping Grandfather to wheel it all the way back to his cabin," Jessie suggested.

Benny sighed. "Well?" he asked. "Is it a clue or not?"

Everyone laughed.

When they were nearly at Hildy's cabin, Andy Watts came up the path toward them. He looked worried. "Well, hello," he said. "I hope there hasn't been another accident."

"Oh, no," Henry said. "We're just . . . exploring."

"We're looking for clues," Benny piped up.

"Clues?" Mr. Watts repeated.

Benny nodded. "All kinds of strange things have been happening."

Mr. Watts listened attentively as the children told him everything that had happened. Then, he said, "My, oh, my! How awful!"

"It's not *that* awful," Benny said. "We like mysteries."

"This is one you may not solve," Mr. Watts said. "It's been going on a while. Other campers have complained about the same things."

"Except for the Changs, we haven't seen any other campers," Jessie said.

Mr. Watts nodded. "Yes, that's what I

mean," he said. "No one stays long. They're afraid to stay."

"Oh, we're not afraid," Benny said.

Mr. Watts edged away. "I have to be going," he said. "Remember, if your grandfather decides to leave, I'll be happy to help. He should be home where he can get his proper rest."

After he had gone, Violet said. "Maybe Mr. Watts is right."

"If Grandfather wanted to go home, he'd say so," Henry reminded her.

"Let's ask Hildy if she knows what's been happening," Jessie suggested.

"She probably won't even talk to us," Benny said.

Hildy was outside her cabin, bent over something on an old table. The children called out to her. She didn't look up. They moved closer to her. She was fiddling with an old kerosene lantern.

"May we speak to you?" Henry asked politely. "Some strange things have been going on — "

"Loud music and lights and missing food," Benny put in.

"We thought you might have seen or heard something that would help us figure it out," Jessie said.

Hildy glared at them. "Imagination pure and simple," she said. "As if it isn't bad enough that my lantern is broken — "

"At least you have a lantern," Benny interrupted. "Someone took ours."

Hildy grabbed the lantern off the table. "Stop pestering me with your silliness," she snapped. She marched to her cabin door. "Go back to the city where you belong! I don't want you here!" She slammed the door behind her.

"You see?" Benny said. "She doesn't want us here."

"Mr. Watts said we should go home, too," Jessie reminded him.

"That's different," Benny argued. "He was thinking about Grandfather."

"We should be, too," Violet said. "We've been away a long time. He might need us."

Grandfather was reading when they returned to camp. "Something happened while you were away," he said.

The children looked at each other. What now? they wondered. They looked all around, but they didn't see anything different.

Grandfather laughed and pointed to the maple tree.

Violet caught her breath. "It bloomed!" she exclaimed.

Earlier, the tree was full of buds. Now, it was full of small tight clusters of green flowers. Other trees seemed to be blooming, too.

"Spring has sprung!" Benny commented.

The night was beautiful, too. The sky was clear and the stars were bright.

After supper, Violet got out her violin. She played several pieces. The one everyone liked best was "Twinkle, Twinkle, Little Star."

Finally, everyone went to bed. They were so tired that they fell asleep quickly. No one heard the loud music that sounded through the still night or saw the lights that cut through the surrounding darkness.

CHAPTER 13

More Trouble

"Yoohoo!" someone called.

"Is it morning already?" Benny asked.

Henry crawled out of his sleeping bag and looked out the tent window. "It's Doris," he told the others.

The children piled out of the tent.

"Well, good morning," Doris said. She set a box down on the picnic table.

"Good morning," the children greeted her.

Grandfather came out of the tent leaning on Andy Watts's walking stick.

"James Henry Alden," Doris said. "Just

what do you think you're doing? You should be resting."

Settled on a picnic bench, Mr. Alden laughed. "Coming to visit an old friend," he answered. "That's what I'm doing. And what are you doing? Hiking all this way when you have a store to run?"

Doris sat across from him. "Andy stopped in late yesterday. He told me about your fall. I thought you might need a few things." She turned to Henry. "There's a bag of ice in there. You'd better put it in the cooler before it melts."

Henry nodded and took out the ice.

Jessie glanced into the box. "You brought pancake mix!" she exclaimed.

"I figured you'd probably used yours up by now," Doris said.

"Somebody took our box," Benny said. "We haven't had a single pancake."

"Someone took your pancake mix?" she said, but she didn't sound too surprised.

"That's not all!" Benny told her what had been happening.

"Hmmm," was all she said.

"We asked your sister about it," Jessie said, "but she just told us to go home."

Doris nodded and glanced away. "Yes, that's what I was afraid of," she said more to herself than to the children. When she saw them all looking at her, she said, "What I mean is, other campers have complained about these very same things."

"That's what Andy Watts said," Violet piped up. "He told us we should go home."

Doris got to her feet. "Maybe it *would* be best if you left," she said. "I'll be happy to help you pack up right now."

"Oh, no, thank you, Doris," Grandfather said. "We're staying."

"Well, I was just thinking of you," Doris said firmly. "It can't be much fun putting up with all that noise and such."

"Can you stay and have breakfast with us?" Jessie asked.

"I have to get back," Doris answered. "I have some . . . business to take care of." At the edge of the camp she turned to face them. "I wish you'd change your mind about leaving, James."

Grandfather laughed. "An Alden doesn't change his mind easily," he said.

Doris frowned. "All right," she said, "but you may be sorry."

"What did she mean by *that?*" Violet asked when Doris had gone.

"Oh, that's just Doris's way," Grandfather said. "She was always very serious."

"We should put her on our list," Benny said.

"List?" Grandfather asked.

"We were trying to decide who could be doing all those strange things," Henry explained.

"We forgot about Doris," Jessie added.

"Well, you can keep her off your list," Grandfather told them.

"But she did act strangely," Henry said.

"She didn't sound at all surprised about the missing pancake mix or any of the other things," Violet said.

Mr. Alden shook his head. "It's not Doris," he said. "She would never think of such things."

The children had a wonderful time playing

in the forest and taking care of Grandfather that day. Only at night when the music sounded and the lights appeared did they think about solving the mystery. But, by then, they were too tired to try to figure things out.

The next morning, Jessie noticed they were low on bread. "That's strange," she said. "I was sure we had enough for a few more days."

"Someone must have taken it," Benny said.

Henry said, "I guess we'll just hike to the store for more."

"Not me," Benny said. "I want to stay here. Grandfather promised to read me a story."

"You and Violet go," Jessie suggested. "Benny and I will stay with Grandfather."

She made a grocery list, and Violet and Henry set off toward the store. They met the Changs in the parking lot. They were packing their van.

"Are you leaving already?" Henry asked.

"Yes, we are," Mr. Chang answered.

"And none too soon," Mrs. Chang added. "With all that loud music, we haven't had a decent night's sleep since we've been here."

Violet was surprised. "But I thought you hadn't heard the music."

"We didn't hear it the night you mentioned," Mr. Chang told them. "We were too tired to hear anything that night."

"There were those mysterious lights in the forest," Mrs. Chang said. "And our food is missing. It's been no picnic; that's for sure!"

"The last straw was finding an arrow holding a message in a tree at the edge of our camp," Mr. Chang said.

"The same things have happened to us!" Violet told them.

"Well, we've had enough," Mr. Chang said. "Be careful. Something is very wrong here."

CHAPTER 14

Hildy Disappears

At the store, Doris was pacing the floor. "You didn't see Hildy anywhere along the way, did you?" she asked Violet and Henry when they arrived.

"No, we didn't," Henry said. "Were you expecting her?"

"This is her shopping day," Doris answered. "She always comes in early so she won't run into any other customers. There's been no sign of her. I'm getting worried."

"And she doesn't have a phone," Violet commented.

100

"No, and I can't leave the store — it's delivery day," Doris said.

"We could stop to check on her," Henry offered.

"Oh, would you?" Doris sounded relieved.

"Sure," Violet said. "But she probably won't want to see us."

"I wouldn't ask you to do it," Doris said, "it's just that . . . well, I'm worried."

With her help, the children gathered the things on Jessie's list. Then, promising to be careful, they hurried off.

Henry and Violet raced into camp.

Breathing hard, Henry announced, "Something's happened to Hildy!"

"Whoa! Slow down," Mr. Alden said to them. "You look as though you're being chased."

Jessie and Benny took the grocery bags from their brother and sister and set them on the table.

"Sit down," Jessie said. "Catch your breath."

They sank to the picnic bench. Benny sat between them.

Grandfather hobbled over and sat down, too. He gave the children time to calm down before saying, "Now, tell us what happened."

Violet started at the beginning. "We met the Changs in the parking lot," she said. "They were leaving because they couldn't stand the music and the other things that have been happening."

Henry picked up the story. "And then we went to the store. Doris was upset because Hildy hadn't come in for her groceries."

"Maybe she'll be in later," Grandfather said.

Violet shook her head. "Doris said today is her shopping day, and she *always* comes in first thing."

"We said we'd check her cabin," Henry told them. "But we wanted to bring the groceries back first."

"And get you two and Watch," Violet said to Jessie and Benny.

"That was smart," Grandfather said.

"There's safety in numbers. I only wish I could go with you."

"Oh, don't worry, Grandfather," Henry said. "We'll be all right."

Benny shot to his feet. "Well, what are we waiting for?"

The four children hurried along the stream path. Watch yapped at their heels.

Hildy's cabin looked deserted. The children approached it slowly. At the door, Henry knocked.

No response.

He knocked again. "Hildy!" he called. "It's the Aldens. We have a message from Doris."

Still no answer.

"Try the door," Jessie suggested.

Henry turned the knob. The door was unlocked.

Slowly, cautiously, Henry pushed the door. It creaked as it swung open.

A few bars of light from the window fell across the cabin floor. Otherwise, the cabin was dark.

"Hildy?" Henry called softly.

He stepped inside the cabin. The others

followed. Watch ran around sniffing.

Pointing to a small table under the window, Benny said, "Look! Our missing lantern!"

A battery-powered lantern stood in the center of the table.

Henry took a few steps forward. "It looks like our lantern all right," he said.

"There are lots of lanterns like that," Violet said.

"But Hildy had a kerosene lantern," Benny reminded them.

"And it was broken," Jessie remembered. She went to the table and picked up the lantern. She turned it over. "It's our lantern, all right," she said. She showed the others the name *Alden* scratched on the bottom.

"Hildy took it!" Benny concluded. "She *is* the one behind everything!"

Henry wasn't convinced. "But our lantern was missing *before* we saw Hildy with her broken one."

"Maybe she already had our lantern here in her cabin," Violet suggested.

"But if she had our lantern, why would

she be so upset about hers being broken?" Jessie asked.

"We don't have time to think about it now," Henry said. "We promised Doris we'd find Hildy."

They went back outside. Benny and Watch ran around the outside of the cabin looking for some sign of Hildy, but they found nothing.

"Maybe she's on her way to the store right now," Violet suggested. "Or already there."

"In that case, we're wasting our time," Jessie said. "Let's go back to camp."

"Not yet," Henry said. "I think we should look around a little more."

"Let's go to Andy's," Benny suggested. "He might know where Hildy is."

They ran over the hill, Watch in the lead.

Andy's place was closed up tight. Even the windows were shuttered.

When the children knocked, there was no answer.

"They're both missing!" Benny said.

CHAPTER 15

The Prisoner

Henry stepped back from Andy's cabin. "The way it's all boarded up, it looks like he's left for good," he observed.

They trooped around the side of the cabin. In back, they saw the wheelbarrow leaning against the wall.

"What's that over there?" Benny asked.

"It's a bale of hay with something on it," Violet observed.

A square white card was pinned to the bale. Painted on it were several circles, one inside the next.

"It's a target," Henry said. "The kind archers use to practice."

"Bow and *arrow* practice?" Benny asked.

Jessie knew what he was thinking. "Just because Mr. Watts likes archery doesn't mean he's the one who put that arrow in the maple tree," she said.

"That's right," Henry agreed. "Someone could have taken the arrows from him."

"Maybe Andy and Hildy are in this together," Benny said. "Maybe that's why they're both missing."

Watch pricked up his ears. He stood listening, and then he loped off toward the cabin.

The children followed him.

"He heard something," Jessie said.

Whining softly, Watch scratched at the door.

Henry knocked loudly. "Mr. Watts!" he called. "Are you in there?"

When no one answered, Benny put his ear to the door.

"There's someone in there," he whispered. "I can hear something."

The door opened a crack. Andy Watts peeked out.

"Oh, children," he said. "I'm sorry I didn't hear you." He yawned. "I was napping."

"We're looking for Hildy," Henry told him. "Have you seen her?"

"No, no, can't say that I have," he answered.

A muffled thump sounded from inside.

Mr. Watts cleared his throat loudly and began coughing.

"I — uh — can't talk to you right now," Andy said. "You run along and I'll see you later."

He closed the door but not before they heard someone yell, "Help! Help! Help me!"

"That's Hildy's voice," Jessie said.

Henry knocked furiously. "Mr. Watts! What's the matter?! What's going on in there?!"

Henry started away from the cabin. "Come on!" he said. "We'll get the ranger!"

Just then they heard a car approaching.

"It's coming from over there!" Benny ran toward a thick stand of trees. He dashed through them, the others close at his heels.

Beyond was a dirt road. The children waved frantically at the oncoming truck. It pulled up beside them and stopped.

Doris hopped out. "What's the matter?" she asked.

"Hildy," the children said at once. "She's locked in Andy's cabin!"

Doris leaped out of the truck.

They all ran back the way they'd come.

Doris pounded on the cabin door. "Andy Watts, come out here this instant!" she demanded. "Or we're going to break this door down!"

The door flew open. "All right! All right!" Andy said. He came outside, trembling.

Doris dashed into the cabin.

The children waited at the door.

Andy Watts paced back and forth. "Oh my, oh my," he kept mumbling to himself.

Finally, Doris came out with Hildy at her side. Hildy looked furious.

"Now, Andy Watts, let's hear your explanation for all of this!" Doris demanded.

CHAPTER 16

The Confession

Andy took a deep breath. "I didn't mean any harm," he said. "I just wanted to give them a taste of their own medicine."

"Who are you talking about?" Doris snapped impatiently.

"Those awful campers," Andy said. "The litter everywhere. They don't care about the forest. They just come here to make noise and mess things up."

"He stole a lantern from the Aldens," Hildy piped up.

"But our lantern is at *your* cabin," Henry said.

"Mine's broken," Hildy explained. "There's no electricity in my cabin. Without a lantern it gets awfully dark. Andy gave me one to use. When I saw your name on it, I began to wonder how he got it."

"So you came over here to question him?" Doris asked.

"I did," Hildy answered. "But when I started asking questions, Andy pushed me into the bathroom and locked the door. I *knew* then that he was the guilty party."

"When did you take the lantern?" Henry asked. "It was there in the morning and, later, it was missing. But Grandfather was at the camp the whole time."

Andy Watts shrugged. "I just waited until he fell asleep. Then I sneaked over and . . . took it. I figured without a lantern, you'd go home."

"You played the loud music, too?" Violet asked.

"Yes, yes," Andy said. "For years, I've had to listen to it. Loud music, loud voices —

any time of the night. The forest is a quiet place. People should respect that. I just wanted to let people know how it sounded. But I never meant to cause Mr. Alden's accident. That made me feel real bad!"

"And the lights?" Jessie asked. "Why did you do that?"

"To scare people away," Andy explained. "That's why I took the food. People get edgy when strange things like that happen. It worked, too. Word got around. Campers have been staying away."

"But how could you take our food when we were right there?" Jessie asked.

"You were difficult," Andy admitted. "I dropped the honey when I heard someone rustling around in the tent."

"That was me," Violet said. "I thought I heard something. I came out to look."

"I just got away in time," Andy said. "And the morning when I took the stew — "

"I saw you!" Jessie interrupted. She turned to Henry. "Remember, Henry? Watch woke me up and then I saw something moving in the mist."

"I was sure you'd catch me that time," Andy said.

"And the arrows? Did you do that, too?" Benny asked.

"That's the first thing I did: turn the wooden arrow that pointed to the ranger's station in a different direction. A few people got so confused, they left. But most people figured it out," Andy said.

"I mean the arrow in the maple tree," Benny persisted.

"Yes," Andy admitted. "I did that, too. When I returned from your campsite, you children were at my cabin."

"That was the morning we found Grandfather in the ravine," Henry said putting the pieces together.

"I only meant to scare you . . . nothing more," Andy said.

"You know, you weren't the first to complain about strange things happening," Hildy said to the Aldens. "I never believed it. Thought it was nonsense. Imagine my surprise when I realized the lantern was yours. And then to find out that Andy Watts of all people was causing so much trouble!"

"She wanted to tell the authorities what I'd done," Andy said. "I couldn't let her do that, could I? They'd put me in jail!"

"And that's why you locked her in your bathroom," Doris concluded.

"I would've let her out," Andy said. "I decided to pack up — get out of here. Go someplace where no one could find me. I would've let her out when I was ready to go." He looked from one to the other. His eyes were sad. "I didn't mean any harm," he said. "Please, believe me."

"Mean it or not, Andy Watts, you did cause harm," Doris said. "You ruined people's camping trips and the park's reputation. Something has to be done about it."

"Oh, I know," Andy said. "It was foolish of me to think of running away. I knew that even while I was packing to go. This is my home. I'd never be happy anywhere else — especially after what I've done." He sighed deeply. "I'll go turn myself in to the ranger."

CHAPTER 17

A Problem Solved

The next night, Doris and Hildy joined the Aldens around the campfire.

"It's hard to believe that Andy Watts caused so much trouble," Doris said.

"I think I understand what he did," Hildy said. "I've felt the same way about some campers. So many of them just don't appreciate the beauty around them."

The children stared at her. She seemed an entirely different person than she was before.

She smiled at them. "Are you having trou-

ble believing old Hildy likes nature?"

"We didn't think you liked anything!" Benny said.

"Now, Benny, mind your manners," Grandfather warned, but he said it lightly, and Benny knew he was amused.

"Hush, James Henry," Hildy said. "I deserved that. I wasn't very nice to your grandchildren — or to anybody for that matter. But I've learned my lesson. These children taught me. Independence is important, but so is knowing people care."

"You know, Hildy," Doris said, "for a while I was afraid you were the one causing all the trouble."

Hildy chuckled. "My own sister!" she teased. "You should have known better. My way of dealing with the campers was to ignore them. Keep my distance."

"Well, things will be different now," Grandfather said.

"They sure will be," Doris said. "Andy did a good thing by turning himself in. Things went easier for him because of it."

"I hope they aren't going to put him in

jail," Benny said. "He might have done bad things, but he's a good man."

"That's exactly what the ranger said," Doris told him. "He came up with a plan to have Andy educate and help campers. It'll accomplish a lot more than a jail sentence would."

"What exactly will he teach the campers?" Violet asked.

"He knows all about the forest," Doris answered. "He'll take people on nature hikes, and teach new campers about safety procedures and anything else they might want to know."

"I hope he teaches them about neatness," Benny piped up. "This place was a mess when we got here."

"I wish we could help," Jessie said.

"You already have," Doris reminded her. "You solved the mystery. Now, campers won't be afraid to come here."

"But we'd like to do more," Violet said.

"Maybe we can," Grandfather said. "Andy mentioned the need for more trees to keep the soil from eroding. I'll donate some."

"We could come weekends and help plant them," Henry suggested.

"That's a fine idea, Henry," Grandfather said. "I'm sure the ranger would approve."

"And the park needs more garbage cans," Jessie said. "That would help people to be neater."

Mr. Alden nodded. "We'll get those, too."

"Maybe we could set up a recycling center with different bins for bottles and cans," Henry said.

"I'll talk to the county officials," Doris offered. "They have special trucks to collect recyclable material."

"I have another idea," Benny said. "Something we can do right now to help some campers."

They all looked at him.

"Roast marshmallows and have some more s'mores," he said.

They all laughed.

"Now, that's what I call an excellent idea!" Grandfather said.

And everyone agreed.

GERTRUDE CHANDLER WARNER discovered when she was teaching that many readers who like an exciting story could find no books that were both easy and fun to read. She decided to try to meet this need, and her first book, *The Boxcar Children*, quickly proved she had succeeded.

Miss Warner drew on her own experiences to write each mystery. As a child she spent hours watching trains go by on the tracks opposite her family home. She often dreamed about what it would be like to set up housekeeping in a caboose or freight car — the situation the Alden children find themselves in.

When Miss Warner received requests for more adventures involving Henry, Jessie, Violet, and Benny Alden, she began additional stories. In each, she chose a special setting and introduced unusual or eccentric characters who liked the unpredictable.

While the mystery element is central to each of Miss Warner's books, she never thought of them as strictly juvenile mysteries. She liked to stress the Aldens' independence and resourcefulness and their solid New England devotion to using up and making do. The Aldens go about most of their adventures with as little adult supervision as possible — something else that delights young readers.

Miss Warner lived in Putnam, Connecticut, until her death in 1979. During her lifetime, she received hundreds of letters from girls and boys telling her how much they liked her books.